SECRETS OF THE MOUNTAIN

For Mum and Dad
~ Libby Walden

For Georgia
~ Richard Jones

CATERPILLAR BOOKS
An imprint of the Little Tiger Group
1 Coda Studios, 189 Munster Road, London SW6 6AW
www.littletiger.co.uk
First published in Great Britain 2018
Text by Libby Walden • Text copyright © 2018 Caterpillar Books
Illustrations copyright © Richard Jones 2018
All rights reserved • ISBN: 978-1-84857-704-6
Printed in China • CPB/1800/0755/1017
2 4 6 8 10 9 7 5 3 1

SECRETS OF THE MOUNTAIN

LIBBY WALDEN   Illustrated by RICHARD JONES

Our mountain watches over us – steadfast and strong.
It holds the secrets of our world on its ancient slopes.

The summit of our home is always
first to greet the dawn.
Early birds unfurl their wings
and take off to the sky…

The snow-topped mountains sparkle in the sun's rosy glow
and the tripping hooves of mountain goats echo on the rock.

As a fresh and cooling breeze rolls down the mountainside,
small pikas stir and scamper, searching for their morning meal.

From the sweeping dewy grass, a wispy mist arises, clearing a path for the morning wanderers.

The midday sun beams down on the woodland edge.

A moose and calf rest peacefully in the warm sunlight.

Further down the mountain,
the forest choir erupts.
Through the dappled branches,
warbles, trills and cheeps resound.

The tracks of bustling animals mark the foothills of the mountain.

A wolverine prowls between the trees as graceful deer stand still –
studying their surroundings in the softening light.

At the base of the peaks, by the water's edge,

the beavers change the landscape; our world is not the same.

The sunset dances on the river's rushing surface,
as bathing bears sense the cool night air drawing in.

The sky is set ablaze once more, burnishing our home.

The evening primrose opens to greet the coming night
and tired creatures journey back in search of quiet slumber.

The blush of dusk transforms the slopes of our mountain,
as the after-dark explorers wake, with a satisfying stretch.

The shadow of the night
frees the foxes and the bats.
Mice scuttle softly
from the scurrying
woodland bandits.

In our moonlit playground,
the bear cubs climb and play,
as dancing fireflies flit and glow
on the night-time breeze.

The flying squirrel performs on the forest's centre stage –
a death-defying acrobat soaring through the silvery arena.

In midnight sky, high above our mountain home,
winged adventurers swirl and swoop beneath the shining stars.

The radiant moon illuminates the rolling mountain plains.
Beneath her pearly rays, the wolf night-watch is on patrol.

Perched on the looming rocks, the mountain lion waits –
watching the horizon for a glimpse of the new day.

Our mountain watches over us – steadfast and strong.

The flash of dawn awakens the early birds once more.

As darkness turns to light, our world is different and the same.

It is eternal and evolving.

It is ancient and alive.

Eagle

Kingfisher

Dall sheep

Pikas

Bats

Black rosy finch

Squirrel

Brown owl

Chickadee

Mountain lion

Blue jay

Wolverine

Wood duck

Mountain goat

Trout

Pygmy owl

Snail

Bobcat

Fox

Beaver

Ant

White-tailed ptarmigan

Black bear

Butterflies